Sharkbait Jones

Stanley Buggles

www.somethingwickedlyweird.com

To read more about Stanley, look out for all the
Something Wickedly Weird books:

The Wooden Mile
The Icy Hand
The Silver Casket

Read more spooky tales in Dust 'n' Bones,
also by the award-winning Chris Mould.

And visit Chris at his website:
www.chrismouldink.com

THE WOODEN MILE

CHRIS MOULD

Hodder
Children's
Books

A division of Hachette Children's Books

For Thomas and Charlie Flather

Text and illustrations copyright © 2007 Chris Mould

First published in Great Britain in 2007
by Hodder Children's Books

The right of Chris Mould to be identified as the Author and Illustrator
of the Work has been asserted by him in accordance with the
Copyright, Designs and Patents Act 1988.

4

A Catalogue record for this book is available from the British Library

ISBN-13: 978 0 340 94477 6

Printed and bound in Great Britain by GGP Media GmbH

The paper and board used in this hardback by Hodder Children's Books
are natural recyclable products made from wood grown in sustainable
forests. The manufacturing processes conform to the environmental
regulations of the country of origin.

Hodder Children's Books
A division of Hachette Children's Books
338 Euston Road, London NW1 3BH
An Hachette Livre UK Company

Admiral Swift

A The Wooden Mile
B The Lighthouse
C The Old Pirate Wreck
D Candlestick Hall
E The Watchtowers
F The Church
G The Village Square
H The Sweet Tooth
I The Grinning Rat

Along the Wooden Mile

In a darkened industrial town, someone weaves unnoticed in and out of the alleyways until he finds the right doorway and forces a package through the letterbox.

This is not the very start of the story. It is simply a convenient place to begin. And you should be warned that when you delve into what has already happened and what lies ahead,

9

you will find this a dark and twisted tale. Good fortune sits in wait around the corner, but grim misadventure lurks sneakily behind.

The package announced itself by landing heavily on the mat. It was addressed to Stanley Buggles. Inside was a short letter and a piece of folded cloth which, when unwrapped, revealed a large silvery-grey key. Not just any old key, mind you, but the key to a rusty cobweb-covered old secret. A secret that wouldn't come out on its own but would need coaxing out of its cage like a frightened bird (as is often the way with secrets).

Stanley read the letter. He read it quietly to himself several times and then he read it out loud to everybody. No one could quite believe it, but there it was in black and white.

Then he held
the key across
both palms.

It was a strange-looking
thing: big and bulky, like
something that would open a castle
gate, and yet intricately decorated with
swirls and scrolls. He placed it back in the
cloth, folded it tidily and put it neatly back in
the envelope with the letter.

Stanley Buggles. A sensitive little chap,
his mother would say. A young wiry-framed
little fellow who would usually be found
wandering the woods alone, climbing the
gnarled old branches just to get a peek at

11

the hawk's eggs, or lying in wait in the undergrowth so that he might catch sight of the fox cubs.

Like all mothers, Stanley's longed to protect him from the perils of the outside world, but she knew she couldn't keep him wrapped up for ever. And anyway, he was no pushover. Oh, no. If ever a kid could look after himself, here he was. Stanley could box like a champ. A proper little jack-rabbit he was, and like all true champs he had the heart of a lion along with that mane of stringy blond hair.

And whilst he had sat one afternoon in the hollowed-out trunk of a tree watching a kestrel circle over an open field, somebody three hundred miles away had sat writing the letter that would change his life for ever.

Penelope Spoonbill
Mayoress of Crampton
Town Hall, High Street
Crampton Rock.

Dear Stanley Buggles,

It is with deep regret that I write to inform you of the sudden death of your great-uncle, Admiral Bartholomew Swift of Candlestick Hall.

As is dictated by the laws of Crampton Rock, the Candlestick Hall estate and further possessions of the aforementioned will pass into the hands of the youngest living relative, you, Stanley Buggles, with immediate effect.

Further paperwork will follow in due course.

In the meantime, in recognition of the circumstances, you are permitted to take care of the front door key, which I enclose. However please do not attempt to visit Crampton Rock until you are in possession of all documentation.

Please accept my deepest sympathy at your loss,

Yours Sincerely,

Penelope Spoonbill

Mayoress of Crampton.

Crampton Rock

Now, first things first. Stanley had no knowledge of his relative, who was, in fact, the perfect example of a long-lost great-uncle. Except that now he was a *dead* long-lost great-uncle, which pretty much spoiled Stanley's chances of getting to know him.

It was decided, when the time came, that Stanley would go on his own to visit the house. He would be put on the train by his mother Marjorie and his stepfather Tristan Fletcher and he would be met by Mrs Carelli, the housekeeper, at the other end. She would be staying on at the house and would take care of Stanley during the summer.

Mrs Carelli informed them that she would be standing on the platform at Crampton Rock station. Mr Fletcher had described Stanley in his letter so that she might know him when she saw him.

'He is eleven
years old
with a pasty
complexion and
a skinny frame.

He will most likely be carrying a large brown case with the words Fletcher & Buggles Manufacturing on the side and looking like he doesn't know where he is going.'

'You can't miss him,' Mr Fletcher had scribbled at the bottom of his letter, explaining that Stanley was 'not really ready for such an adventure at all'.

But as things turned out, he was going to get one and it was about to land on him with one enormous THUD.

Stanley stared through the window of his carriage. As the train thundered along the tracks, the whole world looked completely still. The sun blazed across yellow fields and Stanley wondered what the place would look like.

When eventually the train ground to a

halt, Stanley could see a rickety handmade sign: THIS IS CRAMPTON ROCK. He looked around. From what he could see, the place was deserted and consisted only of the platform itself. Standing just in front of the sign was a stout woman with large ruddy cheeks and a ridiculous hat. Stanley knew this was Mrs Carelli. It must be her, because there was nobody else.

Stanley jumped down from his seat. He had the strangest feeling that despite its dull appearance, there was going to be something very different about this place.

'You can't just get off here, lad. This is Crampton Rock. You needs written permission to get off at Crampton Rock. 'Tis the law of the land. Let's see your ticket.'

Stanley looked up to see a smug-looking train guard grinning at him.

The ticket was in his hand. He held it up.

'I don't need written permission, sir. I'm a resident here. I own a property. I have the paperwork.' It was the first time Stanley had ever said this. He was clutching a file of legal documents at his side, which he had held on to for the whole journey. He waved them at the man, who eyed them suspiciously.

'Mmmmmm, go on then. I don't believe yer, but I'll let yer go this time.' He clipped the corner of the ticket without taking it from Stanley's hand and shuffled away.

As he wrestled his case down from the luggage rack, Stanley muttered under his breath, 'I hope Mrs Carelli is more pleased to see me!'

She was. Well, sort of.

'Hello, you must be Stanley,' she called
when she saw him jump off the train.
'I'll be looking after you at Candlestick Hall.
We can talk later, but for now you'll have to
rush along … tide's coming in.'

And before Stanley could say a word in return, she was walking quickly away on her little feet. Stanley followed on behind, dragging his case awkwardly and wondering why the tide made any difference to anything.

He was about to find out.

As they walked out through the station exit, the ground suddenly disappeared in front of them. There was a sheer drop down to the sea. A stepped footway had been beaten into the earth and was the only way down to the bottom. Then, right where the land met the water, there was a long winding timber footbridge that led, presumably, all the way out to Crampton Rock. It was hard to tell. There were several large rocks obscuring the view and at one point the walkway disappeared through a cave-like opening.

'The Wooden Mile, we calls it,' said
Mrs Carelli. 'When the tide's right up it'll be
gone.' The water was already dangerously
near to the top.

Stanley dropped his case and stood
staring. 'It's incredible.'

'It's only planks, you know. Planks and
nails, that's all,' laughed Mrs Carelli. 'Ain't
nothing new about planks and nails.'

'No, I mean the water,' explained Stanley.
'I've not seen the sea before.'

Immediately he thought of home. In the
dark town where Stanley hailed from, the
coast was a world away. By his bed lay a
tattered old leather-bound book, with a page
that had been thumbed a thousand times.
It held a painting of a rocky beach filled with
every kind of seabird. This was the place he
longed to be.

'Well, you've seen it now, lad. Most likely you'll be fed up of it afore too long, just like the rest of us.' And she blustered onwards, treading the steps down to the water's edge. Stanley followed, dragging his case, fumbling and tripping and all the while trying to take in the view of the sea.

His case seemed to grow heavier.

It had crossed his mind to hurl it down to the bottom, but then he envisaged some terrible accident with Mrs Carelli as the victim and thought better of it.

Shortly they were at the bottom of the steps and making their journey across the wooden mile. The surface was wet and slippery, but Mrs Carelli seemed to glide along. Perhaps she was used to it. It was only when they had passed through the tunnelled cave and out into the open

that the small island of Crampton Rock
loomed down upon Stanley.

A crooked-looking fishing village with
rickety houses and bent chimneys stared back
at him. Littering the harbour and bobbing up
and down on the waves was a crowd of
wooden boats. He was able to pick out the
spire of what appeared to be a small church,
huddled in amongst the rest of the buildings.
To its left, one particular place stood out: a
large house of blackened stone with a crow-
stepped roof. A scattering of little windows
peered out like torchlights from the darkness
of the brickwork.

'There you go, young Stanley. That's
Candlestick Hall.'

He stopped in his tracks. There it was,
the place he had been waiting to see.
The place he had dreamed of. There was

something gloomy and dark about it, yet his heart drummed excitedly at the thought that now the place was his. It was nothing like he had expected: to start with, he could never have imagined it would be so big.

A bird flew from the roof and drew his eye to something else. Something he didn't like. It landed on what he knew to be a gibbet, on a nearby hilltop. He had seen one in a book: a post from which people were hanged in times past. Only, this one held on to a rounded cage, and in it were the spindly skeletal remains of a single human life.

Mrs Carelli had glanced back and noticed him looking.

'Don't worry, Stanley,' she said kindly. ''Tis only the remains of some rotten scoundrel.'

Stanley shivered. 'Who was it?' he asked.

'Pirates,' she answered. 'Sometimes we gets pirates here. They pass by this way and we would rather they didn't. 'Tis only there to serve as a warning.'

'Is it real?' asked Stanley. He had never seen a dead body before.

'Oh, he's real all right! From the tip of his head to the soles of his shoes, he's real,' she laughed and then, seemingly unconcerned, she walked the last few boards up to the harbour wall where some of the villagers were waiting.

'But what happened to him? How did he … die?'

Too late: she was already out of earshot and had begun talking to somebody.

Stanley looked back and watched the waves washing over the timber walkway as it slowly began to disappear. There was no going back. Not now!

Candlestick Hall

Stanley was about to step up on to the harbour when a huge man in a cap and trenchcoat stopped him. He introduced himself as Lionel Grouse, Keeper of the Rock, and he was accompanied by the Mayoress, Penelope Spoonbill. She was dwarfed at his side.

'I'm afraid I'll need to see your papers, son.

You can't step on to Crampton Rock until I've seen your deeds,' announced Mr Grouse.

This was the second time someone had stopped him and he wasn't even there yet.

Stanley put his case down and fingered through the paperwork. He was panicking that he had lost what he needed.

The water began to wash around the soles of his shoes.

'I'm getting wet, sir. Is there a chance I can step up on to the wall to sort out my papers?'

'Sorry, lad, I need to see the documents first.' Mr Grouse smiled, and waited.

The water washed around Stanley's toes. He found his letter from Mrs Carelli. That wasn't it. The water washed around his ankles. He found his copy of Admiral Swift's will. But that wasn't it. He began to grow worried. Had he dropped them?

The water was rising more and more quickly. It would be up to his knees shortly and he wasn't sure he would be able to swim.

Suddenly he held it right there in his hand.

'Here,' he said, relieved and very wet. 'I have it.'

The man held out his arm. 'Welcome, Stanley,' he said, and pulled him up on to dry land.

Stanley was stopped short in his tracks by a frail woman, clasping his arm tightly.

'Don't step out on to the moor, Stanley. It's no place for a young boy.'

She was shuffled to one side by Mrs Carelli. 'Please, give the boy a chance.' A handful of villagers herded the old woman to one side and through Stanley's excitement he temporarily forgot her words.

He dropped his case and ran swiftly to the house, scattering water as he ran and squelching in his soggy shoes. He turned the key in the door and stood in the hallway.

It was hard to take in all at once.

'Make yourself at home, Stanley,' said Mrs Carelli. 'I shall be right there in the kitchen if you need me.' She pointed to a long room at the far end of the house. 'Get something dry on your feet, have a look around and I'll make us something to eat. Oh, and don't forget, your case is still sat by the harbour. It'll not grow legs.'

Stanley had left and returned again in two minutes flat.

He was blown away by the size of Candlestick Hall. It was so grand, and he had only ever lived in a small house with tiny rooms.

It would take him the whole summer just to explore.

The hallway was bigger than his whole house back home. It was full of curious objects, most of which hung on the walls or stood in glass-fronted display cases. A moose head hung over the door and beside it was a stuffed monkey with its mouth wide open, showing sharp teeth. Below, a suit of armour stood staring back at him.

There was a sitting room at the front, looking down on the harbour. The fireplace was so big Stanley was able to stand inside it. The bones of some huge fish were fixed over the mantelpiece.

At the back of the sitting room, a short dark passage took him back out into the hallway and he was back at the staircase. Halfway up it there was a break, with a tall window. Stanley ran to the window and looked out across the harbour to take in the view across the water. It was a rare sight for anybody, but for a boy who had never seen any more water than you could get into a bathtub, it was unbelievable. He went to the ledge and watched the waves roll back and forth.

Upstairs was much the same. Room after room after room, some furnished, some empty. Most with the shutters pulled over the windows, sitting in darkness with blades of light piercing through the screens and cascading across the bare floors.

Stanley chose a room at the front where he could watch the sea from his bed. He opened his case and scattered some of his things across the bed to leave his mark, then he carried on exploring.

One room held him captive. At first it seemed to be just a room full of cupboards.

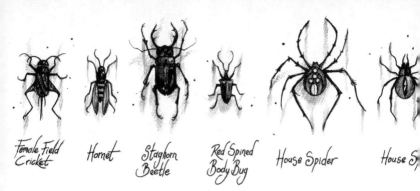

Female Field
Cricket   Hornet   Staghorn
Beetle   Red Spined
Body Bug   House Spider   House S

But when Stanley pulled open one of the drawers, it was laid out neatly with every possible species of bird's egg, labelled in beautiful handwriting.

He opened another. Butterflies. And another. Shells. On it went: insects, animal bones, fossils, old letters, drawings, plans of the house. Here he would spend some time. He knew that.

After a while he returned to the ledge and watched the sea until Mrs Carelli called him for supper.

There were two places set at a small table

in the kitchen. A large pie sat in wait for him. He suddenly realized that he was hungry: he hadn't eaten since breakfast.

He sat down and when Mrs Carelli joined him he asked, 'Can you tell me about Admiral Swift?'

She seemed taken aback. 'Oh, your Great-Uncle Bartholomew. Well, there ain't much to tell really. He was retired from the navy. Spent most of his life out on the water. He even died out there, minding his own business sitting peacefully in his fishing boat. Shame that was.'

'How did he die?' asked Stanley. Mrs Carelli sighed and said some other time she'd tell him, but that now he wasn't to worry himself with morbid details and should eat up his pie and settle in.

Bivalve Mollusc

Shell

Limpet

But worry about morbid details he did, and after supper he decided it was time to explore the garden and possibly visit the churchyard and the Admiral's grave. He'd seen the churchyard out the back when he'd been exploring the upstairs rooms earlier.

'Make sure you're back before dark comes in now, Stanley,' Mrs Carelli said. 'Crampton Rock is no place for youngsters after the light goes. I'll be waiting for you.'

Stanley made his promise, stepped out through the front door and round the back under the arched buttress.

The garden was mostly grassed and without borders. There was a line of yew trees running from top to bottom with their foliage tidily clipped into circular shape. A high brick wall framed the lawn and at the very far end was the gateway leading to the moor. He went closer, staring at the overgrown hinges and realizing the gate had long been out of use. In the distance he could see crooked hand-painted signs dotted across the landscape.

He remembered the words of the old woman on his arrival.

Stay off the moor

'And on this rock I will build my church.' This was engraved on the large stone outside the gates to the church. It was surrounded by old and crumbling gravestones. The grass was long and unkempt and the door looked to be bolted shut. A low stone wall ran around the outside. The gates were unhinged and leaned awkwardly at an angle. Stanley crept over the wall and began to read the inscriptions on the gravestones.

HERE LIES JASPER TINDELL,
GOOD CITIZEN OF CRAMPTON ROCK.
1812 – 1871

And another:

AT YOUR FEET LIES MARY CRUMP,
REST IN PEACE. 1660 – 1703.

And Stanley's favourite:

HERE RESTS ELIZABETH GREEB
1748–1800
PLEASE DO NOT STAND WHERE IT HURTS.

The light was already dropping. Stanley
remembered Mrs Carelli's words; he must get
back or she'd be coming to find him. He had
wanted to see if there was a stone for Admiral
Swift. Maybe another time.

Mrs Carelli was at the door with a worried
look on her face. 'Come on, young Buggles,'
she said. 'Time you were inside.'

Soon after, he was upstairs when a bell rang
out in the village. He watched in wonder as
the streets cleared in a matter of minutes.
People filed indoors like marching lines of ants.

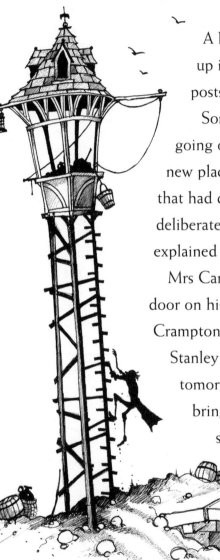

A handful climbed up into the look-out posts.

Something was going on in this strange new place. Something that had definitely and deliberately not been explained to Stanley.

Mrs Carelli locked the door on his first day at Crampton Rock and Stanley wondered what tomorrow would bring. He would soon find out!

3

the Pike

Mrs Carelli was nowhere to be seen the next morning when Stanley eventually woke up and dragged himself down to the kitchen. He'd found it difficult to get out of bed and had lain there till quite late, mesmerized by the view of the sea. When he did get downstairs it was nearer to lunchtime than breakfast, and there was a note on the table from Mrs Carelli, saying that she had gone into town and would be back before it was dark. Of course she would, he thought. Darkness put a stop to everything on Crampton Rock, or so it seemed.

The previous day he had noticed a corridor that ran under the back of the staircase. At the time he hadn't explored it. Now, he saw that it led to a part of the house he had not yet seen. The walls were panelled with wood and the way was dark and narrow. At the end, next to a doorway, was something mounted on the wall in a long glass case. He went closer.

It was a very large fish. Its body was long and slender and it had sharp needle-like teeth. It was not like any other fish he had seen. There was a brass plate on the wooden surround. Stanley read the inscription.

'A preserved 22 1/2lb pike caught by Admiral Bartholomew Swift in Crampton Springs, 1827.' Was it real? It didn't look it. Its surface was shiny and new, its glassy eye lifeless in its socket. The case was decorated with pebbles and shale and bits of reed.

And then, as Stanley stood and stared, a voice came from the glass case and the fish spoke to him.

'Tread carefully, Stanley. Stay away from William Cake and beware of the lady who lives in the water.'

That was it. Nothing more, nothing less. Did he really see it move? Did he really hear it? Who on earth was William Cake? And who or what was 'the lady who lives in the water'?

Stanley spent the whole afternoon going backwards and forwards to that fish.

He would tap on the glass, he would stand
and wait. He would even try to talk to it …
but not a word would the fish say.

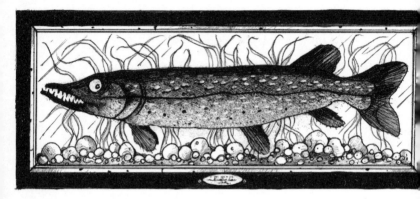

But Stanley remembered the words. He
even wrote them down. What were they
about? When he realized the fish wasn't
going to speak again, he decided he had most
likely been daydreaming. After all, he had
been through a lot lately and the chances of a
fish (and a dead one at that!) speaking to him
were fairly remote.

He was distracted by the noise of the clock sounding out the hour. He had heard it the day before, but not taken the time to look at it. It was so big that Stanley was sure he could climb inside it, and just when he had managed it, Mrs Carelli walked through the door! She stood right there next to the tall case, removing her hat and coat. Stanley froze on the spot, but Mrs Carelli didn't notice him. She even looked up at the time.

'Are you there, lad?' she cried out, then headed off into the kitchen.

Stanley sneaked out and followed on behind her. 'Good morning, Mrs Carelli.'

'Aahh, good AFTERNOON, young Master Buggles. I take it you slept well?' she enquired.

'I always sleep well,' announced Stanley. 'It is the thing I do best.'

She smiled and without looking up she informed him that he was the master of the house and if he should choose to sleep during the day then she was not entitled to argue. Then they both laughed and Stanley had a good feeling inside. Mrs Carelli was OK, he had decided.

And then he spoiled it.

'I was thinking I might pop out again after dinner,' he said. 'It's time I found my great-uncle's grave and paid my respects.'

Mrs Carelli turned and looked him straight in the eye, pointing at him with her wooden spoon. 'Stanley Buggles, I'm here as your legal guardian. That means I has to look after you, not throw you out in the night like a farmyard cat. Graveyard visiting should take place in daylight hours and not the hours of darkness.'

'Sorry!' he returned, taken aback by her

abruptness. She really didn't like the dark at all, did she?

'Come on,' she continued, a bowl of soup in each hand. 'You can bring that bread, up there on the worktop.'

And soon they were talking away again like old friends. But Stanley felt the urge to ask the morbid question once again. 'Er, how did Great-Uncle Bart die?'

'Oh, here we go again,' she laughed. 'Well I suppose you're entitled to know. Mind you, it ain't nothing pleasant so I hope you've got a strong stomach, young Buggles.'

His ears pricked up expectantly.

'Your Great-Uncle Bart was attacked, Stanley. Something out in the night took him. A crazed animal of some kind. He was in a terrible state, he was. We didn't even know if it was him at first. I knew he had a tattoo of a scorpion on his forearm so they looked and there it was.'

'Why didn't they just look at his face to see who it was?' enquired Stanley innocently.

'I'm afraid, Stanley, that … well, his face wasn't there. What I mean is, well … his *head* wasn't there … Now come on and eat up,' she insisted. 'That's enough questions for one mealtime.'

Stanley stared at his soup. He wasn't hungry any more.

A slice of Cake

Stanley longed to quiz Mrs Carelli about the pike and its strange, mystical warnings, but he could not bring himself to tell her it had spoken to him. She would think him mad. Perhaps she knew – she had lived here all these years looking after Admiral Swift's home. On second thoughts, maybe he should just forget the whole thing! He had already told himself he was daydreaming.

In an attempt to rid himself of his thoughts, he decided to spend some time away from the house and get to know Crampton Rock a little more.

Mrs Carelli had promised to arrange for him to spend a day with Lionel Grouse, out in his boat. Stanley had discovered that Lionel's grand title of Keeper of the Rock simply meant that he lived in the light-house. He had twice brought fresh fish to the house since Stanley's arrival and seemed a friendly sort.

Stanley was going to need as many friends
as he could get.

He was already missing
home. He had spent that
morning describing
everything

in a long letter to his parents. It contained a wonderfully detailed drawing of the house, and a map of Crampton Rock.

With the letter in his pocket, he set off to find the post box. He wandered down to the harbour on his way. The tide was out and he had taken an interest in the seabirds since he had arrived. He sat and watched the oystercatchers sweeping the beach for shellfish. Further out the plovers searched hungrily in the rock pools.

'Pass me them there lobster traps, young lad,' came a voice. A white-haired old fisherman looked up from the bottom of his boat. The traps were laid in rows along the harbour wall. Stanley passed down the strange basket contraptions and before long he was talking to the rest of the men in the harbour and had spent a good hour or so helping them ready their boats with nets and rods.

When the tide meandered in and lifted the boats, they sailed off and he made his way alone along the streets.

It was the first time Stanley had wandered into the village, and when he saw the maze of alleyways and crooked shops and houses he wondered why he hadn't ventured further from the house much earlier. Shortly he found himself outside a sweet shop. A wooden sign hung on an old iron bracket:

The sign was old and weathered, which made the teeth look yellowed and rotten. He stared through the glass at the window display.

A small round mechanical boy in glasses fed sweets into his mouth from a paper bag. Stanley could see the cogs winding back and forth. There was something spooky about it. Perhaps it was the movement, or maybe the strange face of the child, which seemed to look right through him. But he could not resist a step inside the shop.

An old bell tinkled as he pushed the door. Once inside, he was faced with shelf upon shelf and jar upon jar of every kind of treat. Candy sticks were laid row upon row across the long counter. Humbugs, cinnamon sticks, liquorice, lollipops, bubble gum and mint balls stared at him through their glass containers.

Suddenly a small hunched man appeared. 'Can I help yooouuuu?' he asked in a funny voice, then disappeared again just as quickly, without waiting for a reply.

'Errr ... yes,' Stanley began.

The man appeared again as if from nowhere and leered over the counter.

'Yesss, what is it, lad? What do you want?'

He was dressed in a long coat, wore tinted glasses and was bald with wisps of hair that shot out at the sides. His huge hands were turned out flat on the counter. Stanley noticed that they were hairy and that his fingernails looked long and sharp.

For the second time, Stanley was going to experience something very odd. The man removed his glasses and came closer to Stanley. But the pupils of his eyes weren't circular.

They were long slits that ran from side to side like sheep's eyes, and the coloured part was a scary yellow.

Stanley was so shocked he jumped back and knocked a display of toffees crashing across the floor. The man remained very still and looked on silently until Stanley had cleared up the mess.

'I'm very sorry,' Stanley said, picking them up as fast as he could and bundling them back into the basket. He felt obliged to buy something, so spent a little longer eyeing the contents of the shop before he picked something and left.

On his return to the house, Stanley wandered into the kitchen and greeted Mrs Carelli, who was in her usual spot preparing something.

'You've been out all day, lad,' she said. 'Have you not eaten?' And before he could answer she looked at the bag of sweets in his hand.

'Don't tell me you've been in that sweet shop, Stanley?'

'Well, yes,' he began, 'in fact something strange happened and I—'

But she cut him off. 'Listen to me, Stanley Buggles, and listen good.' She paused as if she was preparing what to say in her head.

'Sweets is bad for you. I don't want you in that place again. You hear me?'

'They're only humbugs,' he quizzed. 'They won't kill me.'

'STANLEY.' Her voice became louder. 'You has two ears and one mouth. Use them in the same proportions, will you?'

'Well, OK,' he said calmly. 'I was none too keen on the place anyway.'

'Here,' she said. 'You'll do better to get this down you.' She threw an apple in his direction. He cupped it in both hands and took a bite.

After tea he sat by the fire and pondered over Mrs Carelli, trying to make up his mind about her. That was twice she had blown her lid. He was going to have to tread more carefully in future.

Now Stanley was not the type to go ignoring strict orders. Oh no, he was no fool. As his stepfather would have said, he knew which side his bread was buttered. But there was a slight problem. What with helping the fishermen and the incident in the sweet shop, Stanley had forgotten to drop his letter into the post box. Trouble was, the post was only collected once a fortnight. It would be gone at six o'clock prompt the next morning and be on the boat by half past. The chances of Stanley getting out of bed in time were zero, and he had promised to get in touch with home as soon as he could.

He would have to go back. He looked outside: the light had dropped. There was no chance of being let out, not at this time.

'We're a bit low on firewood,' he shouted upstairs to Mrs Carelli. 'I'll just nip out to the

garden.' He took the full basket with him
so he could return with it. By the time she
had opened her mouth to remind him it was
the middle of summer, he was already out of
the door.

Mrs Carelli frowned to herself. She would
interrogate him on his return and he had
better not be long.

In less than two minutes, Stanley was
standing in the dark village. The light was on
in the sweet-shop window and he realized
the mechanical boy was still working. It was
quite a sight in the darkness of the street and
he stood trance-like watching it repeat its
sequence, over and over.

Then he was distracted by something
behind him. He froze. He could feel
something at his heels but almost
didn't dare turn around.

He gasped a sigh of relief. It was just a stray dog, lank and skinny and missing a back leg.

And then, for the first time, Stanley noticed the name over the shop door.

It said:

Proprietor: WILLIAM CAKE

A distant howl drifted through the air and the dog scampered off into the gloom. Stanley felt a chill rattle through him.

The noise of a loud bugle came from overhead. Someone had spotted him out in the dark from the harbour watchtower and was sounding the alarm. A voice shouted at Stanley but he couldn't hear what was being said.

He turned home, quick on his feet. Finally slipping in through the front door, he ran to the glass case under the stairway and stared at the pike.

'Please tell me more!' he whispered. But Mrs Carelli must have heard the alarm and seen him come through the door. She was hunting him down.

'STANLEY BUGGLES, I want a word with you! I've warned you about spending too long out in the dark more than once now, and if you're not careful I'll resort to locking you in your room!'

It was only a small fishing village, thought Stanley. What was so bad that he couldn't step outside the door after dark? He climbed the staircase and sat in his room, looking out of the window. The dog trundled past awkwardly on its three legs. A fantastic moon hung over the harbour and sprinkled yellow light upon the fishing boats.

'There is something wickedly weird about this place,' said Stanley through the open window.

He lay on his bed and opened a book. But before he had even begun to read, he had fallen asleep, the book flat on his face. And the forgotten letter to his parents settled deep into his coat pocket.

5

Randall Flynn

The following morning, Stanley was
wandering through the village and although
he was becoming accustomed to peculiar
happenings he was surprised to cross the path
of another three-legged dog. No, it *wasn't*
the same one. It was smaller and scruffier.
It couldn't have been *more* different from
the first one. And anyway, this time it was

the front leg on the left and not the back leg on the right that was missing. This is what his mother would have described as 'too much of a coincidence'. And indeed it was. In fact, the more he thought about it the more he was sure he hadn't seen a dog with every limb intact since he'd arrived.

Just when he was pondering over this he realized he was standing outside The Sweet Tooth again and that Mr Cake was peering out through the window. But the dog distracted him, circling round his feet and fussing over him. Stanley ruffled the hair on its head and scratched its chin. Its coat felt rough, and a small black patch was circled over one of its eyes.

'C'mere, Silver,' came a shout. A spindly-looking character with long dark hair and a chiselled face was beckoning his dog,

tapping his thigh with the flat of his hand and whistling in short bursts through his teeth.

'Come on, Silver, 'ere boy. S'all right, lad, he won't hurt you. But I'd stay away from that place if I were you,' he said, nodding his head towards the shop. 'It'll only bring you trouble.'

'You mean the sweet shop?' asked Stanley, who by now was trotting alongside the man, trying to match his pace. 'Do you know Mister Cake then?'

'Only well enough to stay away from 'im.'

'What do you mean?' persisted Stanley. But the man was not for talking much.

'I'm just warning yer, lad, that's all. C'mon, Silver.' And he was off again.

'What now?' said Stanley to himself. He had to find out more. He was in the middle of something and he didn't even know what it was.

He wandered aimlessly, watching the fishing boats in the harbour, and found himself up on the hill where the inn stood. A sign swung in the breeze over a small wooden door studded with iron nails. The Grinning Rat. Suddenly he noticed Silver again, scratching around in the doorway.

Stanley peered through a small window. The spindly-looking man was sitting in a corner, staring into a drink.

Stanley had an idea. Perhaps if he waited, the drink would loosen the man's tongue! He shot inside. 'I'll walk your dog for you, mister.'

'Not you again!'

'I don't want nothing for it,' he said. 'I just like dogs.'

'All right, lad. Don't be too long, mind.'
He smiled, showing a row of blackened pegs,
as he handed him a tattered length of rope.

Stanley made sure he was gone for a good
couple of hours. On his return, Silver's owner
was slightly the worse for wear. Six tankards
were lined up on the table. Stanley sat down
and handed back the lead.

'I'm sorry I was so long. He got away!'

The man hit the dog and it shot under
the table with a whimper. Stanley stared at
his feet.

'What were you telling me about Mister
Cake?' he asked, as if the long-haired man
had been halfway through telling the story.

The man looked Stanley straight in the
eye and knitted his brow. He leaned closer to
him and Stanley could smell the ale on his

breath. There was a small tattoo on his neck: a mermaid with a curled-up tail and long hair. He took a shifty look around

the room and then steered his eyes back again.

Stanley's plan had paid off.

'The name's Flynn. Randall Flynn. But you didn't hear any of this from me, right.'

Stanley nodded. He didn't want to interrupt the man's flow.

'Old William Cake ain't no ordinary shopkeeper. Fact is, he ain't much of a shopkeeper at all. Ever seen any kids in that there sweet shop, 'ave yer? No, I thought not. Come to think of it, I bet you ain't seen nobody in there at all!'

'Why's that then?' enquired Stanley, his eyes growing bigger and rounder and his ears pricking up.

'People round 'ere are scared of 'im. They reckon old Cake has something of the night about him. Came to this village to try and settle down with a cosy little business and live the peaceful life, but somewhere along the way he didn't quite manage it. Just can't help himself.'

'I'm so sorry, Mister Flynn sir, I just don't know what you're saying!' admitted Stanley.

'The man's a werewolf, lad. A creature of the night. Call it what yer want.'

'Do you mean … are you talking about … (he struggled to remember the word) … *lycanthropy*? The transformation of man into wolf under a full moon?' (Stanley was a mine of information on this subject. Back home he had read every book he could find, and he thought he knew all there was to know about werewolves.)

'Don't believe everything you read in books, lad. Books is bad for you.'

'What do you mean?'

'Tain't nothin' to do with full moons, lad. You been readin' too many fairy tales. Werewolves is brought on by nightfall. As sure as night follows day, that thing will prowl these moors and stalk that town, full moon or not.'

A grisly-looking landlord leaned in on the conversation as he plonked another mug of ale on the table.

'In certain parts and places they are what darkness brings,' Flynn added. 'I'm afraid, young man, that *this* is one of those places. Ain't yer seen those hairy arms with hands like shovels hung on the end? Ain't yer seen those eyes? That ain't normal.

'One minute he's a little old man with a bad back and a stiff leg, and in the next breath, he's down on all fours, racing through the night with teeth like razors.'

'How could you know all this?' asked Stanley, a huge lump in his throat. Although he found the story ridiculous, it somehow made sense of the things that troubled him. The emptying of

the streets at sunset. The people in the
watchtowers.

And of course, the grim death of poor
old Admiral Swift.

'Tell you how, lad. 'Cos I seen it with
my own eyes, that's how. You see that
wrecked-up old boat on that there beach?
That belonged to the biggest band
of crooked rotten scoundrels that ever
lived.

'Pirates, they was. Every last one of
'em. Came ashore late one night two
years ago, drunk as newts, staggering
about in the village square. Until they
met old William Cake, deep in the middle
of one of his funny turns. Bent double,
full of hair with huge claws and saliva
dribbling down his chin in a fevered
hunger. Polished off the lot of 'em, he did.

Well … all apart from one, anyway.'

'Who was that?' enquired Stanley, his throat dry.

'Me!' said Flynn. He pulled up his shirt cuffs. A deep scar ran around both of his wrists.

'Had to have these sewn back on,' he continued. 'Took 'em clean off, he did.

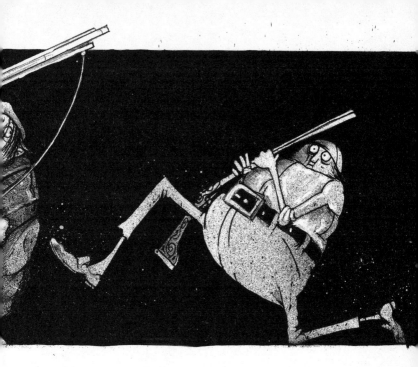

I'm lucky to be alive.'

By now Stanley was shaking at the knees.
'You, you're ... a pirate, and he's some kind of
werewolf, you say.'

'Keep yer voice down, young 'un. The likes
o' me ain't too popular round 'ere. They'll
have me off this island before you can say
Crab Soup, and I got plans to stay.'

79

'How do I know you're telling the truth?' asked Stanley, whispering.

Flynn's eyes sharpened and his nostrils flared. His face came closer again. Stanley gave way and moved backwards a little, wishing he hadn't opened his mouth.

'Don't just take my word for it, lad. Look around you. There's an awful lot o' clues about. This place is empty on a night for a start. Nobody wants to stagger home drunk when there's wolves about. Don't tell me you haven't noticed that bell ringing at dusk, the streets clearing, the villagers in the look-out posts. Ain't yer seen all those sheep carcasses out on the moor? They weren't eaten by wild rabbits, y'know. There's a lady in the village, claims she shot a wolf one night, wandering about in the square. Next morning Cake was limping about like an old woman.

'And why do you think all the dogs have got missing legs? They're the ones that got away!'

Just then Silver sniffed at Stanley's leg under the table and touched him with his cold wet nose.

Stanley jumped so far he fell backwards on to the floor. He made his excuses and left the inn. 'Thank you, Mister Flynn,' he said. 'I'll see you again maybe.'

Stanley set off across the hill with his head in a spin. He would make his way back to the house across the moor without going down into the village. He was safe whilst it was still light. For once he was keen to get home before the night drew in, and it was nothing to do with Mrs Carelli.

And as he walked, he wondered.

Something struck him, something the pike had said. 'Beware of the lady who lives in the water.'

And he recalled the mermaid on Flynn's neck.

The more Stanley thought about William Cake and Randall Flynn, the more ridiculous the whole thing seemed.

'*Randall Flynn is just a drunkard who wishes he'd been a pirate and makes up tales when he's had a few and William Cake is just … well, he's just a funny little old shopkeeper and people always make up stories about funny little old shopkeepers and that*

Mister Flynn should be ashamed of himself.'

This is what Stanley imagined Mrs Carelli would say about the whole thing – except that he had promised not to say a word about what had been discussed, so perhaps he would never know.

Up until now Stanley could have chosen to ignore the bizarre incidents that were going on around him and stay out of trouble. But circumstances were about to decide that he became very deeply involved.

This is how they unfolded.

He was looking out over the harbour when Silver appeared with a piece of paper in his mouth and placed it in his lap before scampering off.

The Grinning Rat
- Noon -
BE THERE!
Flynn.

Well, it wasn't a party invite, that was obvious. He decided he had better be there and in the next half-hour he was climbing the hill that steered up to the inn.

The inn was an old building with beams and a steep roof. The windows were small and the sign that hung over the door bore a picture of a fat-faced pirate. He had a patch over his eye and a large knife held between smiling teeth.

Randall Flynn was not alone.

'Meet some *old friends*, Stanley,' laughed Flynn.

On Flynn's right-hand side, slumped into a corner, was a slant-eyed, mean-looking rogue. A recently inflicted wound sat over his left eye.

'This is me old mate Bill Timbers. The most wicked of pirates. He's made a thousand men walk the plank.'

Bill Timbers didn't greet Stanley. He just fixed an unnerving stare on him and kept his arms folded.

On the other side of Flynn was a larger, rounded man.

'And this 'ere is old Sharkbait Jones.

A brave fellow. The victim of a frenzied shark
attack, but still 'ere to tell the tale.'

Sharkbait Jones had one arm missing and
a wooden leg on the same side. He was a

terrifying sight. Somehow he had
managed to salvage the bones of his
left arm and hand, and they were sewn
on to his jacket in the correct position. He
was slightly more friendly than Timbers, but
there was still something Stanley couldn't
trust in that smile.

He kept making terrible jokes about being 'half the man he used to be'. Stanley didn't find this amusing, but he had decided to pretend that he found it as funny as they did, and joined in their laughter. He wasn't sure if being polite was the done thing around pirates but, nevertheless, that was what he was going to do.

He had never seen such dried-up faces. Their clothes were like rags and they smelled of salt water. When they were close, their breath was like dead shrimps and alcohol mixed together. Their skin was a grim purplish-blue colour and the whites of their eyes were yellowed. Their teeth were all blacks and browns, in higgledy-piggledy rows like crooked tombstones.

Now, Stanley figured that old Flynn was not really one for making friends, and if he

had brought him to The Grinning Rat it
wasn't because he wanted him to walk his
dog again. Stanley figured that this was
going to lead to something he didn't like.

He was right.

'So you're a pal of old Hangman Flynn,
are you?' asked Timbers.

'**HANGMAN** Flynn?' squeaked
Stanley.

'Oh, I didn't tell yer that bit,' grinned
Flynn, and they all three burst out into
raucous laughter, spilling their beer
and frightening Silver, who cowered by
their feet.

'Listen, lad, I know you knows
different but as far as anyone else is
concerned we're all shoemakers, yeah,'
insisted Timbers.

'Cobblers?'

'No, I'm serious.'

'Yes, I know, a cobbler is another name for a shoema— it doesn't matter. Carry on.'

Stanley sat trembling. He was hanging on to his nerves and telling himself that bravery was about facing things when you knew deep down that you were scared. He breathed deeply and gritted his teeth.

'Come on, Stanley,' he muttered to himself.

'Listen, lad, we ain't ere to mess about,' said Jones. 'We want our revenge on Cake. We want rid of 'im, but we need your 'elp.'

'How's that then?' Stanley asked. He couldn't help thinking how ridiculous it seemed. Three vicious pirates, all wanting rid of one man – yet they needed the help of an eleven-year-old boy! His heart sank. It was bad enough that he was mixing with pirates. Now he was about to *become* one!

'We've noticed you're staying at Candlestick Hall,' said Timbers.

This was a bad start for Stanley. They knew where he lived. The last thing he wanted was drunken pirates knocking on the door. Mrs Carelli would hit the roof.

'Only for a short while.' Stanley dodged the issue. There was no point in denying it. 'I'll be heading home before too long.'

'There's a tasty-looking pistol hanging over that mantelpiece,' Timbers continued.

'The one in the glass case with the silver bullet. Only one way to kill a werewolf, Stanley. And that's with a silver bullet.'

Stanley shuddered. How did they know the inside of the house? The thought of them snooping around sent a shiver winding down from his head to his feet.

'You mean you want me to get you the gun and the bullet and then you'll shoot the wolf and then I can put the gun back and it will be all over and you'll leave me alone?'

'Almost,' said Flynn '... but not quite! Y'see, we got a little problem.'

As he spoke they all three

94

turned out their hands (or what was left of them) on to the table.

'There ain't one of us 'ere capable of firing a gun no more.'

'I can't bend these fingers since my hands were sewn back on,' announced Flynn.

'And I got caught out playing with dynamite,' said Timbers, grinning and staring with a raised eyebrow. His index and middle finger were missing from both hands.

Stanley noticed that Jones' right arm and hand was fully intact.

'Don't laugh,' said Jones, 'but I'm left-handed. Always was, always will be. Can't get used to using this damned thing. Just don't trust myself with a gun. Especially in the company of wolves!'

'What's yer aim like, lad?' asked Flynn, and they all burst into a sinister cackle, sending the dog scurrying off into a far corner of the inn.

Stanley wasn't happy. If the rumours were true, surely it was safer to get rid of William Cake in his harmless form than it was to go around shooting werewolves.

'Don't work like that,' snapped Timbers, who didn't take to the boy disagreeing with him. 'Werewolves 'as to be got rid of when they're werewolves. The human part of them survives. And anyway, what's it gonna look like, you gettin' caught shooting little old men? Not everybody believes Cake is the one. You could end up looking at life through a barred window.

'You're far better off being a hero. Ain't nobody *else* around here gonna do it, that's for sure.' And their laughter grew louder.

Stanley was still trembling with nerves,

but he was angry at what was being put
upon him and he couldn't resist asking one
question.

'How come none of those watchmen have
shot that wolf?'

'It's a good question, Stanley,' replied
Flynn, almost as if he knew it was coming.
'But I got a good answer. These folk is fishing
people. They uses nets and rods to catch
what they're after. They're simple people
with simple ways. That gun up at your place
is probably the only one on the island. I
bet most of 'em ain't never even seen one.
All those watchmen do is keep a look-out
and make sure everybody's inside. They
needs your 'elp, Stanley. You gotta get up
pretty close to shoot somethin' right between
the eyes.'

Stanley knew that despite their good humour

they were serious. And now he had the following choice. Risk being killed by a vicious and bloodthirsty wolf, or be lynched by angry vengeful pirates.

This really was turning into a terrible business.

7

Through the Telescope

A few days later, Stanley was sitting at the
dinner table playing with his pie and mash.
He could feel Mrs Carelli's eyes fixed on him,
and knew what was coming.

'What is it, Stanley, what's the matter?'

'Nothing,' he answered, so unconvincingly
that she pressed him further.

'Yes there is, young Buggles. You normally

eats like a horse but I ain't seen you eat more than a crumb for days *and* you've gone quiet. *Especially* quiet.'

She did have a way of weeding things out of him, but Stanley would have to keep hold of this one for now.

'OK, OK,' he started. 'You're right … You see, the truth is, well, I'm just missing home a bit. I mean, I love it here you know but, well, I've never been away from home before. I know it's stupid.' And he started to tuck into his meal, making sure he cleaned the plate.

Mrs Carelli's face dropped. 'Stanley, I'm here for you night and day should you need me. Not just for cooking and cleaning. I know how it feels to miss someone. Years ago I lost my husband. Victor, his name was. Went on a fishing trip out at sea, he did and never came back. A bad storm took his boat.

We found bits of it washed up on the beach.'

Stanley had stirred some feeling deep inside her and discovered something he had not known.

'I'm sorry,' he said. He could think of nothing else to say.

Just as the light was dropping, Stanley stepped out into the rear garden. He had left some gardening tools on the lawn and was about to bring them inside. Mrs Carelli had asked him to do it that morning, but as usual he had gone off on some adventure around the house and forgotten to do so.

With his hands full, he turned to head back indoors when he felt a three-fingered grip fasten around his throat. It was Bill Timbers. Stanley dropped the tools at his feet.

'You all right out there, Stanley?' came Mrs Carelli's voice from the kitchen. Timbers glared at him with a stare that told him not to make a fuss.

'I'm … fine,' Stanley gasped.

'You ever seen one of these?' Timbers asked, pulling a huge knife from a binding around the bottom of his right leg. It was broad, with a bone handle and a blade that would shave the whiskers from a fly.

Stanley couldn't manage an answer. The grip around his airway had tightened and Timbers held the tip of the cutter against the point of his nose.

"Tis a fishing knife, lad. Y'know the kind. Just right for removing the gizzards.

Tain't no use against wolves and other such midnight nonsense, but all the same I still uses it when I'm going about me daily business, if yer get me meanin'.'

And he went on to explain to Stanley that just because he couldn't fire a gun it didn't mean he wasn't capable of doing some *irrepairable damage* to whoever fell foul of him.

'Tick tock, tick tock, Stanley,' he sneered, turning the blade. 'Time is running out. You better make full use o' your time on Crampton Rock now, or you'll miss yer chance and I 'as a way to deal with timewasters.'

'Stanley, have you brought those tools in yet?' came a familiar voice.

In a blink, Timbers was gone, scuttling over the wall like a long-legged lizard.

Stanley picked up the equipment that lay scattered around his feet and turned inside.

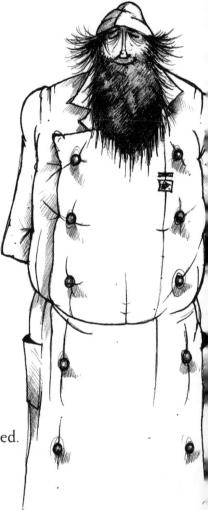

The next morning, Stanley was up and around in good time after a sleepless night. As he was dressing himself, he heard Mrs Carelli answer the door to a deep voice.

'Come in,' she said. 'I think he's awake.'

His heart quickened.

He peered over the balcony but he could only see Mrs Carelli.

'I won't keep him all day,' he heard the voice say.

Stanley breathed a sigh of relief. It was Lionel Grouse from the lighthouse, come to take him fishing. Mr Grouse was all beard and smiles, with wild orange hair and a weathered face.

'Come on, young Stanley,' he grinned. 'I'll make a fisherman of you yet.'

Stanley had not expected to feel sick on the boat, but it was the first thing that hit him as they breezed across choppy seawater. They dropped lobster traps as they ventured out and when they had gone some distance, Mr Grouse prepared the fishing rods and they cast off into the sea.

Stanley was beginning to enjoy himself again. For a while all that business of wolves and pirates had disappeared. This was real life. Out on the open water, taking in the sea air and getting away from it all.

Up ahead a tall rock speared majestically out of the water. A few trees grew in the small space at the bottom and water crashed relentlessly around the edge.

'What's that?' asked Stanley.

'The North-East Needle, we call it,' answered Lionel. 'Nothing much there except a small cave and a flock of gulls now and then. But that rock is twice the height of Candlestick Hall.'

Stanley peered upward at the tallest point, looming over them like a stooping giraffe. It looked as if it could crash down at any moment.

Suddenly he jumped: something was pulling furiously on his line! Mr Grouse stood at his side, guiding him at the reel. But no, it was gone. It had wriggled free and he soon discovered that whatever it was had taken the hook, line and sinker with it.

'There's some big fish in these waters, Stanley, bigger than you can imagine,' said Mr Grouse. He turned to Stanley and put the rod in its rest. 'Stanley, we need to talk. I didn't bring you out here for no fancy fishing trip. Sit yourself down.'

Stanley's expression dropped into a serious wide-eyed stare as he perched on a low seat.

'I want to talk to you about your Great-Uncle Bart. He was a good old friend o' mine. Oh, he'd seen some rough 'n' tumble times at sea, but in his later life he was a peaceful, gentle man. Bart liked to fish at midnight, Stanley.

He were getting out of his boat one night and didn't quite make the journey home.

'Rumour has it that our resident werewolf was to blame. Except some folks don't like talk of werewolves. Don't like to admit we have a problem, so they cover it up, you see, just like all bad doings get covered up one way or another. I guessed you'd pick up on it before long, so I wanted to put you straight. Mrs Carelli ain't too keen on telling you such things, though.'

'I knew it,' gasped Stanley. 'I knew the werewolf was to blame.'

Stanley was daring himself to question Mr Grouse about William Cake, only he was struggling to find the right way to say it.

'That there lighthouse you live in, Mister Grouse. I bet you can see a lot from there?'

'Oh I can, lad, yeah I can.'

'Can you see the streets and houses if you look back in at the Rock? Can you see The Sweet Tooth?'

'Better than I'd like to, Stanley. Sometimes I can see more than I want to.'

Just then the sky turned black and a crack of thunder could be heard far off in the distance.

'Time we wrapped up and called it a day, I think. There's a storm blowing in.'

'I know,' said Stanley. 'I can feel it.'

When they reached dry land, they shared out their catch and Mr Grouse escorted Stanley to the door with a full basket of fish.

'Don't forget, no mentioning you-know-what to you-know-who,' he instructed. 'She don't like talk of wolves.'

Stanley reassured him and said goodbye, thanking him for the fishing trip. He closed the door on the day as the rain came and darkened the cobbles on the street.

He had decided that, pirates or no pirates, if Crampton Rock had a werewolf that had killed his great-uncle and he could do something about it, he would. But he had to be sure. He couldn't just assume someone was a werewolf; that was ridiculous. So he put together a plan that would ensure the truth.

Two days later, Stanley had cunningly managed to get an invite to stay overnight with Mr and Mrs Grouse at the lighthouse – so that he could join Lionel in looking out for the fishing boats. This is what his mother would have called *a weak excuse*. The real reason, of course, was that Stanley wanted a good view of William Cake at midnight when the moon was full.

Somehow, Stanley felt that Lionel knew what he was up to. Mrs Grouse had put him in the room right at the top where the views were open and clear. A telescope was mounted on a stand at the top of the staircase.

Darkness poured over Crampton Rock. Stanley had never had such a fantastic view of the island. From here he could see the endless stretch of the ocean, but he could also look back at the twinkling lights of the village and the boats in the harbour. In customary fashion, the streets emptied with the fading light and the blue bulb of the moon ran along the rooftops and rippled among the housing.

It was crisp and clear, but a misty sea fog flowed around under the streetlights as the town clock struck twelve. Stanley was sitting at the edge of his rickety old bed, his head resting on the stone sill. He had taken the telescope and held it in both hands.

Slowly, he raised it to his keenest eye and aimed towards the crooked building that was the sweet shop. The moonlight pierced downwards and picked out the upstairs windows at the back. They were barred. Surely this was a telltale sign. Maybe Cake had tried to stop himself from breaking out of the house when he turned into his midnight form.

All was quiet. Stanley moved his sight downwards to see that Cake's doorway was smashed to pieces and lay in smithereens around the dustbins of the back alley. A howl whistled through the cold night air. Stanley's heart quickened in excitement – but it was too late. The wolf must have burst out through the door. It was hungry tonight, he thought.

After a while, he fell asleep with his face pressed against the window. He awoke to see a long black shadow disappearing up on to the moor. He'd missed it again!

He forced his eyelids open and eventually, in the early hours of the morning,

his patience was rewarded. The man in the
harbour look-out was asleep with his head
resting in his hands, as a formidable shape
of blackened fur with a sleek and slender
body stood in the square, prowling like a
majestic lion.

'That's no ordinary wolf,' whispered
Stanley.

The arch of its huge back must have been
nearly two metres from the ground. The
creature snaked around the gable end of a
building and dug its snout into a pile of
empty boxes, seeking desperately for some
source of nourishment.

Stanley quickly picked up the telescope.
Now he could see the wolf so closely,
the scope shook in his hands and
he lost sight several times
out of sheer panic.

The shape headed
into the harbour
just as Flynn's
dog trotted
around the
corner.

Stanley held his hand over the end of the telescope … but it didn't stop him from hearing the distant helpless yelp that came from Silver as he breathed his last breath.

The wolf disappeared again and Stanley watched nervously. Where was it now? He heard a noise behind him. Breathing. He looked round and in the darkness of his room he could pick out a huge shape with a mass of hair.

'Quite a sight, isn't it?' came a voice.

It was Lionel. Phew!

'Is it really him?' questioned Stanley.

'I'm afraid it is, lad. I've seen it too many times. Now you know the dark secret of Crampton Rock. You just make sure you stay in after dark, Stanley, that's all I ask. And don't go getting any fancy ideas. We don't need heroics.'

'I won't,' he answered, and the lie stuck in his throat.

Stanley climbed into bed to salvage the
sleep he could from what was left of the night.

In the morning, Stanley woke just before first
light. He peered out through the window.

To his surprise, he saw William Cake

sneaking back down from the moor across the village square. He was naked and he darted quickly from one hiding place to another as he went. As he inspected the shattered rear door of the shop, he held his head in his hands. Then he shot inside, eager not to be seen.

Mrs Grouse made Stanley the most amazing breakfast – but though it was not like him at all, his nerves had got the better of him and hunger was the last thing on his mind. He pushed the food down.

An hour later he had grabbed his belongings and was making his way back to the hall.

As he reached the door, a piercing scream came from inside. It was Mrs Carelli, he was sure. He tore through the front door; by the time he had reached the bottom of the staircase, he had envisaged every possible kind of horror. Suddenly, before he could imagine anything else, the scene unfolded in front of him.

Mrs Carelli stood on a stool, her face white and a feather duster in her hand.

'Ooooh, Stanley, I'm sorry. I've never seen such a monstrous hairy beast in all my life. Could you kill it? You're not scared, are you?'

Stanley stood in bemusement.

'There lad, in that corner. Hurry up, will you?'

It was a spider. A relatively *small* spider. Stanley cupped it in his hand, dropped it on to the step and shut the door.

A Can of Worms

Stanley was staring at the gun with the silver
bullet. It was mounted in a case on smart
blue baize.

Mrs Carelli was out and Stanley was free to
spend a while pondering over his plans. He felt
Admiral Swift looking down at him from his
portrait. He had a kind face, and Stanley knew
he would have liked his Great-Uncle Bart.

Scared as he was, he knew he must do the deed, not only for the sake of Crampton Rock, but also for his great-uncle.

Just then, Flynn's face appeared at the window and Stanley jumped out of his skin. Flynn rapped on the glass with his fist.

'Where's my dog, Buggles? I ain't seen it all night.'

Stanley felt terrible about what had happened to Silver, yet he was loath to admit what he knew. Why should he?

'No idea,' he squeaked.

'Tick tock, tick tock,' Flynn laughed. 'No time to lose, Stanley. Get rid of the wolf and let the sheep live in peace.' He drew his forefinger across his throat, and left.

Stanley looked at the pistol again. He had never shot a gun before. He would need to be close: one silver bullet meant one chance.

Earlier, when he had been snooping around in the upstairs room that was filled with curiosities, he had found a small booklet. Inside was every detail, from loading the pistol and shooting it to dismantling it and cleaning it. Stanley had not yet got his hands on that gun, but already he knew it inside out.

That night, Stanley ventured out again. Mrs Carelli had been late to bed and it was well into the night before he could be sure she was asleep. And then he had to take the pistol from the case in the dark and load it before he left. So by the time he was outside it was later than he had hoped.

He stood in the back garden. Flynn had told him he should have a better chance of finding the wolf on the moor. It was two

124

o'clock and a chill wind sent a shiver rattling through him. He trembled uncontrollably and wasn't sure if it was through cold or fear. Most likely it was both.

With the pistol tucked inside a small bag, Stanley vaulted the gate that led out on to the moor. The night was clear and bright and Stanley couldn't help thinking how good it felt to be out at such an unearthly hour. As he ventured further, the foliage grew more closely around him and he pushed on carefully through the silhouettes of leaves and branches. With each step he became more careful. If he blew it that was it. No more Stanley. No more Crampton Rock.

In the distance he could hear the sea crashing against the rock on the far side of the island.

He could roughly make out where the land ended. The sea bobbed on a purple-blue horizon. All was peaceful. Perhaps tonight the wolf was resting and Stanley could live to fight another day. Stanley almost forgot why he was there, it was so beautifully peaceful.

'Not tonight,' he thought to himself, turning back towards home.

He hoped Mrs Carelli hadn't been woken when he left; he didn't fancy an argument with her at three in the morning.

He was almost at the gate. He thought that he was safely back. But there was no way of preparing Stanley for what came upon him next.

Up ahead, he saw a light pointing its way across the moor. Who else was out? No one ventured on to the moor, not at this hour.

Moving swiftly, Stanley perched inside the dense growth of a nearby bush. His eyes opened wide in the dark, but still he couldn't see who it was. His heart beat hard in his ears. Someone was wheezing and gasping, lantern in hand, on to the moor.

Suddenly it came clear. Stanley knew that limping stride and that hunched stoop. It was William Cake. Perhaps he escaped on to the moor when he knew what was coming, to put himself out of harm's way.

Stanley thought he had dealt with fear already. He was about to learn that he hadn't.

A drifting cloud gave way to a crescent moon and a silvery-blue light picked out Cake's pathetic figure. He was struggling, bent double in pain. Stanley was tempted to jump out and help him – but he stopped short when he realized what was happening.

Cake dropped on to all fours. A crunch and crack of bones echoed over the night as his limbs began to elongate into the monstrous shape of a formidable beast. His knees bent backwards and his spine grew up in a huge arch.

Stanley recoiled in horror at the sight of Cake's jaw mutating into a great snout

with huge teeth. It was an ungodly sight.
Within a brief moment of change the
hulking figure of a great wolf stood before
him. It breathed heavily from its efforts
and a pile of torn clothes lay at its feet.
A spluttering of spittle dangled from its
gasping jaw. And it was between Stanley
and home.

Stanley turned and fled the way he had come. Much as he had wanted to face the beast and fire the shot perfectly, somehow he couldn't. He shoved his way back through the foliage, tripping on stones and small humps of earth. He could hear the rush of the sea again as he neared the cliff. Looking back, he saw the wolf's evil eyes coming closer.

He raced through darkness, forcing his way past the blackened shapes of stalks and tendrils. Spiny roots and branches reached out like arms and legs to trip his feet. Behind him the monster chased hungrily, its hot breath now blowing at his ankles. Stanley scarpered like a frightened rabbit, bobbing from left to right.

Then he tripped headlong and downward. Over the edge he went, in what felt like slow motion. Suddenly the sea came into view and his body was careering over the cliffside.

Somehow, and with a strength that came out of desperation, he grabbed on to a tree root that jutted out from the sandy edge. His body jolted hard against the drop, suspended like a fly in a spider's web.

He looked up to see the wolf leer silently forward. Its bright-yellow eyes glowed ghost-like through the darkness; its huge tongue dripped saliva on to his forehead. Its head was so large that he thought it might swallow him whole.

The beast pulled back its lips to reveal all of its powerful, dragon-like teeth. But it couldn't quite reach him! Just maybe he could reach inside his bag and take out what he needed. With one free hand he fumbled and panicked, but at last he could feel the cold metal and knew that he held the pistol in his hand.

'Come to Daddy,' said Stanley. He raised the gun out of his bag and, holding it closer than close, he sent a bullet hurtling between the wolf's eyes.

KABOOOOM! The sound was deafening. Stanley's bony frame shook like a leaf on the branch that held him. The pistol recoiled violently and jumped from his hand, crashing to the rocks below.

In what seemed like slow motion, the beast was thrown backwards. Its legs flailed aimlessly and a limp tongue hung from one side of its mouth. Stanley listened for its hefty weight crashing to the ground, but the sound of the sea crashing on the rocks drowned out the thud as it hurtled head first into a nearby thicket.

It was all over.

Well, when I say all over, I mean almost.

Stanley was still helpless, hanging from
the cliff face.

He was there for what seemed like hours.
Eventually, he heard Flynn and his men
discussing what to do with the wolf. They
must have been watching from a look-out
post.

Stanley called out, and over the side of the
cliff came three ugly faces.

'Well, well, well. If it isn't our pint-sized
hero, Stanley Buggles.'

And with only sixteen fingers and five
thumbs, they hoisted him up and dusted
him down.

'That be a job well done, Stanley. You go
on home now and get yer beauty sleep, it's
growing light already. We'll finish up here.'

Stanley didn't need any more coaxing.

He was gone. Over the moor he ran, half of him elated and the other half scared to death he was about to hit big trouble back home. How he would explain the missing gun he didn't know.

Finally home, he sneaked up the staircase, treading carefully over every board. When he got to his room, he climbed into his bed still clothed and gave a sigh of relief.

'Ahhh, look who's here. It's the return of the midnight cowboy.'

Mrs Carelli was sitting on his window seat. She was looking out to sea and didn't bother to turn around as she spoke to him.

'Been a long night for you, Stanley. You'll be needing some sleep, I guess.'

'Errr … I guess so,' answered Stanley, still in shock.

She turned to him, furious. 'You've no idea what you've done, Stanley, no idea. Now the trouble will really start. You've opened a can of worms, you have. While that thing was still alive, those idiots was gripped in fear along with everyone else around here. Now it's gone they're free to roam around at night and do what pirates do. Loot and pillage and turn people's lives upside down. And do you know what they wants most of all? They wants what they think is in this house. *Your* house.'

'*What?*' said Stanley, bemused.

'Listen to me, young Buggles, and listen good. Your Great-Uncle Bart was no admiral. Sure, he was a good man and all that but he'd never been in no navy. He was a pirate. A buccaneer. Came here to settle down. Had enough of the sea life and villainy and all that. But he brought trouble with him, you see; once a pirate, always a pirate. Where trouble goes, trouble follows.'

'What?'

'Stop saying *what* and listen.'

Stanley was sitting with his ears pricked up and eyes wide open.

'Now I'll guess you ain't never heard of the Ibis?'

'You mean the bird? An ibis is a wading bird.'

'Right, well yes it is, but that's not what I mean. This is different. It's an ancient amulet, one of the most precious in the history of looting and pillaging. Stolen a thousand times, buried on every island the world over and passed through the hands of every rotten crook and scoundrel that ever lived to tell the tale. Now I don't know much about it, Stanley, but one thing I do knows is that it's here.'

'Where?'

'Somewhere here, in this old place. And now that Cake is gone, they will come in the night and they will tear your house apart.'

'Oh,' said Stanley. 'I ... I see.' He hesitated.

'What is it, Stanley? What you thinking? Come on, let's have it out. Let's get to the bottom of all this.'

'Well ... why have they never come here during the day? If they're fearless pirates and they're so desperate, they wouldn't bother about *when* they came, would they?'

'Let me tell you something, Stanley. Those *fearless pirates* ain't got a brave bone in their pathetic little bodies. They're villains and they act like most villains do. Tough when they've been at the beer, brave when there's a few of 'em, fearless when it's dark and there ain't no one around. But deep down they ain't made of much. All the same, what they wants is here and they're desperate. They won't give up until they find a way.'

'Why can't they just be thrown off the island?'

'It's a nice thought, Stanley, but Flynn owns the old windmill on the far side of Crampton Rock. He can stay as long as he's alive, along with his guests. Most people think he's just an old shoemaker. I can't prove he's a pirate. Can you?'

'Well, no. But maybe they just wanted revenge on Cake and that was all. Maybe they'll never try and get in the house.'

'They already have.'

'What?'

'Oh yes, Stanley. Your brave pirate heroes have darkened your door once before. After your Great-Uncle Bart died, before you came, they were here late one afternoon after too much beer.

'Came across the moor they did, creeping through the garden. Came right through that back door, into the kitchen.'

Stanley sat bolt upright. 'And what then?'

'That's when they learned not to mess with Mrs Carelli, Stanley. This old lady ain't no pushover.'

A smile broke over Stanley's face. 'Tell me more.'

'I'd just mopped the floor, so needless to say that lopsided lump, Jones, was on his back as soon as he came through the door.'

'Then what?' asked Stanley, already breaking into laughter.

'Well, I'd just got my bread fresh out the oven and I was stood there wondering what to do and, well, it just came naturally.'

'What did?'

'I've always had a good punch, Stanley. Ever since I was younger. So I dug my hands into those fresh crusty loaves and used 'em like boxing gloves. My goodness they were hot, but it worked a treat. Knocked those two lily-livered landlubbers flying, I did. Mind you, I was sickened. Them granary loaves was wasted.'

After all Stanley had gone through and everything he had just heard, the thought of

Mrs Carelli bashing Randall Flynn and Bill Timbers with two brown loaves sent tears of laughter streaming down his face.

Mrs Carelli's face had told her tale very sternly, but suddenly she saw the funny side. She looked at Stanley and burst into a giggle. Shortly they were both laughing uncontrollably at the crazy story of the pirates and the loaves of bread.

'I guess that's why they would rather you were tucked up in bed when they came,' he said, trying to straighten his face.

And somehow Stanley knew that, come what may, and despite the troubles ahead, he would never see the three buccaneers in quite the same way again.

Dreaming

In the short time that Stanley slept before
daybreak, he dreamed of the mermaid.
She came to life and swam around his head,
singing beautifully. But the sound haunted
him and he stirred restlessly, tossing and
turning in his bed.

He saw row upon row of granary loaves.
And then the wolf was standing over his bed.

He woke with a start, praying for the end of the night.

When the morning finally arrived, he was keen to know if there was any evidence of the previous night's adventures.

He wandered down to The Sweet Tooth. The door was wide open and the sign in the window read 'Open as Usual'. Intrigued, he peered inside.

There was Mr Cake, like nothing had ever happened, busying himself behind the counter.

Stanley retreated slowly, his mind crazy with thoughts. What had he done? Who had he shot? Somebody else?

'Stanley Buggles, Stanley Buggles. Come on in, I have something for you.'

Before Stanley could turn and run, Cake was right there upon him. He held Stanley by the arms and stared into his face.

'I want to thank you, Stanley. Your stay
here has changed my life. Here, you must take
these,' he said, and thrust a huge bag of sweets
into Stanley's hands. 'And if ever I can help
you in return I should be pleased to do so.'

Cake was different. His eyes were a pale
blue and his pupils were back to normal.
There was a mild expression in his face. A
terrible scar sat right in the middle of

his forehead. A scar that suggested the shape
of a bullet. A silver bullet, perhaps!

That night, Stanley dreamed
of the pike.

A single frosty eye glared at him closely, and as he watched he could see his own reflection in its pupil. He could hear the rush of the water. And then it spoke again.

'Fear not, Stanley. When you are gone, I shall hold your secret safely.'

Over and over went the words from the pike. When Stanley eventually woke, he found that he was standing right there in front of the pike's glass case, at the dead of night.

What did it mean? The only secret Stanley held close at heart was the terrible business with the wolf.

'I don't have a secret,' he said sleepily.

Confused by yet more senseless dreams, Stanley rubbed his eyes and went back to bed, where he slept until late morning.

Making Plans

The seed of an idea planted itself in Stanley's head as he sat at the breakfast table. The idea grew and grew until, in a short space of time, it was a glorious foolproof plan that he was proud of.

He knew that it wouldn't be long before the pirates were on to him, one way or another. He'd made it safe for them to move at night.

He had a feeling they were waiting and watching from somewhere.

First things first, thought Stanley, and without breathing a word to Mrs Carelli, he set off to make devious arrangements with Mr Grouse down at the harbour.

An hour later he returned with a wicked grin on his face. 'Phase two,' said Stanley, as he sat at the kitchen table with a large piece of paper and a clutch of pens and brushes.

If there was one thing Stanley could do well, it was draw. He spent the rest of the day sketching a map. When he had finished he took what was left in the teapot, stained his artwork and dried it out again. Then he crumpled it, folded it, stood on it, dragged it through the dirt, burned the edges and did anything else he could to it, until it looked like a perfectly scrappy piece of old parchment.

Stanley looked out from his window across the harbour to enjoy the remains of the day. All was quiet. The fishing boats were back, and seagulls picked at scraps in the fading light. It was a crisp, clear evening and the onset of dusk had just about cleared the streets. In time, Stanley thought, people would realize there was no longer any danger.

Three old ladies in cloaks and bonnets were heading along the harbour wall. One carried a basket of flowers. Another hobbled on a stick. Someone shouted to them from a look-out, 'Hurry along, ladies.'

'Oh yes, thank you,' came a weak croak of a voice.

The trio were making their way to the door of Candlestick Hall.

Perhaps they were friends of Mrs Carelli's.

Stanley ran downstairs, and had opened the door before they could knock.

What a sight. Three ugly mugs with eyes bulging out of their bonnets, crooked teeth and bad breath. Stanley realized it was *them*. Here already! They couldn't even wait until it was safe to break in, such was their enthusiasm.

Stanley knew he ought to be scared. But to his surprise, the overwhelming feeling of amusement at the three rogues dressed as women made him laugh out loud.

'Good evening, young sir, we is from the church and would like to talk to you about our good work wot we 'as been doing,' said Jones in a feeble, high-pitched voice.

'Oh yes? Did you really think we wouldn't know who you are?' Stanley chortled.

'Let us in, Buggles. We still got business

with yer,' whispered Jones, changing his tone back to a gravelly rasp.

'And look, I brought flowers for the good lady of the 'ouse,' Timbers claimed, as he took a withered bunch of heather from his basket. Stanley could see the blade of the fish knife underneath. It caught a chink of light from the hallway and twinkled, glaring at him in warning.

Stanley moved to shut the door, but like a flash Timbers swapped the bouquet for the knife and pierced the blade into the wood, pushing the door back.

'Ain't no one quicker than old Bill Timbers with a knife, Stanley, so why don't yer let us in before I ties you up with yer own gizzards.'

The three pushed their way in and Stanley backed up into the drawing room. Timbers kept watch by the door to the kitchen corridor, peering nervously around. Perhaps, Stanley thought, he was waiting for a baguette to spear him from behind. Or maybe a shower of bread rolls that would rain down and knock him to the ground. He concealed his laughter, but his shoulders were shaking.

'Someone there, Stanley?' came a familiar voice echoing down the long staircase.

'Only ... Mister Grouse,' he replied. 'Brought some fish. I'll take care of it.'

Mrs Carelli was tidily out of the way. Stanley knew she could handle the pirates, but she would scupper his plan. Sure, a right hook with a crusty bread loaf would keep them at bay, but they needed dealing with permanently.

'Good boy, Stanley. We got you well trained, 'aven't we. Now listen. We needs to 'ave a look around the old place. So keep 'er upstairs, will yer?' Flynn eyed the room up and down. 'Yer Great-Uncle Bart 'ad somethin' that belonged to us and ... well, we needs it back.'

'And what would that be?' enquired Stanley.

'Oh, just a small worthless trinket to be honest, lad. But ... yer know, it was my mother's brooch an' all that so I'd like to 'ave it back.'

The three of them were snooping around, eyeing the place over, lifting lids and opening drawers. Stanley hated bad manners. And he knew just how to get their attention.

'Pirates don't usually dress up as old women and threaten folk with knives just to get their mother's brooch back,' he began. 'What you're after isn't here, I can assure you.'

'An' how would you know that, Buggles?

We knows this place better than you do. Just let us find what we're after and we'll be gone. Nobody gets 'urt and it's all done an dusted. Or if you want we can come back later when everyone's asleep. We don't mind.'

Stanley felt the urge to toy with them for a while. It was safe. He had the answer they needed, so they would have to be careful with him now. He had all three of them in the palm of his hand. They wouldn't admit that, but they knew it.

'You know, it's my favourite breed of bird,' Stanley announced.

'What?' asked Timbers.

'The ibis,' Stanley carried on. 'A magnificent wading bird common to many parts of the world. The scarlet ibis is my favourite, though I've never actually seen one, except in a boo—'

That did it. All three turned on him immediately. Timbers' knife was back in his hand and pointing into the Adam's apple on Stanley's neck before he could blink.

'WHERE?' they all said at the same time.

Stanley slowly drew a deep breath and stared right at them. They backed off, six yellowy eyes staring at him. He could have had them begging on their knees had he wanted, they all knew that.

'It isn't here,' said Stanley.

'Liar,' said Flynn. 'Don't mess with us, Buggles, I 'aven't paid you back for getting rid o' my dog yet.'

Stanley ignored Flynn's remarks. He took the map from the breast pocket of his shirt.

'Ever seen this before?' he asked, knowing full well they hadn't. 'It was Great-Uncle Bart's.' He held it open, but not near enough to be scrutinized. 'Kept it under lock and key, he did. Was a long time before I found it. Shows a small island. North-East Needle. Doesn't mean anything to me. Could be anywhere.'

'Pass it 'ere,' snarled Jones, hobbling forward.

Stanley held the map over the flames of the fire. 'Mister Jones, your manners are appalling.' All three shrieked and jumped forward. He held it there.

'I don't want your precious Ibis,' said Stanley. 'I want you villains away from my property and out of my hair. So be good pirates and do as I tell you, and we'll all get what we want.'

Stanley was feeling good, until the edge of the map singed and burned his finger, and they all laughed at him.

'Shhhh,' he insisted. Mrs Carelli would hear them.

'Cocky little snipe, isn't he?' said Flynn.

Mrs Carelli was making her way down the staircase. They would have to go out of the back door. Stanley herded them down the long corridor to the kitchen.

'Stanley, what's all that banging?'

'Nothing.'

It was Jones's wooden leg on the polished floorboards.

He stepped outside with them.

'Listen,' he started, 'I got a boat for tomorrow. I'm heading out there alone.'

'Yeah, and we're comin' with yer!'

'You can't,' he insisted. 'It'll look suspicious. I can't be seen with you three.' He paused a moment. 'OK, but you'll have to get on board early and hide in the three barrels. You'll have to do it at night. At least you're safe in the dark now. I'll be leaving at six a.m. Look for the *Blue Oyster*. That's the boat.'

'Aye, aye, Captain Buggles,' laughed Flynn, and the three old ladies clambered over the gate and back across the moor.

Stanley sneaked back inside.

'Where did you put the fish?' asked Mrs Carelli.

Stanley was thinking on his feet again. The basket was still on the floor with the flowers thrown to one side.

'Sorry, did I say fish? I meant ... flowers,' he said as he gathered them up and gave her the basket. 'Mister Grouse brought you flowers.'

'Oh,' she said, and her eyes pored suspiciously over the withered heather. 'Stanley, are you up to something again?'

'Not at all, Mrs Carelli,' he insisted, and put a confused look on his face to reassure her.

'Good. Now get them doors bolted before we have unwanted visitors.'

11

The North-East Needle

At five-thirty sharp the next morning Stanley was locking the front door. He dropped the key inside his shirt where it hung on a length of string. He had told Mrs Carelli not to expect him before early evening.

He ran down to the harbour, eager to know if the pirate crew had joined his treasure mission. When he reached the boat

he was instantly reassured: snoring was
coming from the three barrels, each one in
turn making its sound, like a small orchestra
of zeds. Empty rum bottles littered the
bottom of the boat. The pirates must have
been there all night, he thought. Ah well, so
much for not acting suspicious – they could
have awoken the whole neighbourhood!

As Stanley was casting the boat off, he

heard the sound of the cabin door being unlocked. 'Morning, Stanley, is all going to plan?' came a whisper.

'Brilliantly,' answered Stanley.

There was Lionel Grouse, with a hammer and a hessian bag filled with nails.

'Your three friends were here at three o'clock. Straight from the inn, drinking and singing like something was worth celebrating.

At one point they tried to break into the cabin, but they were so drunk the three of them ended up on the floor tied in a knot.'

'What about the look-outs? Weren't the pirates spotted?'

'Nah, the look-outs must have dropped off by then. They usually do. They're not much use after midnight – they take a drink to calm their nerves and eventually it gets the better of 'em.'

'Why is there a table leg in the boat?' asked Stanley.

''Tain't from no table, lad. 'Tis Jones's wooden limb. Couldn't get into the barrel without losing something, so he took it off and I have to say he caused a great commotion in the process.'

Lionel put a row of nails in his mouth and, taking the hammer in his hand, he tapped the

nails into
the tops of the
barrels. The
snoring continued,
becoming louder when
Stanley removed the
round wooden plugs from
the sides.

'Best let some air in,' he chuckled.
'I don't expect it's too pleasant in there.'

They set off into the open sea, and
after a good while they found themselves
approaching the North-East Needle. Lionel's
expert mastery of the boat allowed them to
navigate through the rocks and hook on to the
edge of the island. Gulls cried out deafeningly
above, crowding the cliff's lofty point.

The barrels were rolled up a small ramp and dumped unceremoniously at the base of the cliff. Lionel secured them to each other with a length of rope and then wrapped it around a withered old tree to stop them rolling back into the drink.

'We don't want no sea scum washing up on our beach, now do we, Stanley?'

Stanley took the fake map from his pocket. He threw it on to the water's surface and watched the colour wash out of it as it disappeared into the greeny blue.

The two of them spent the rest of the day fishing and laughing out loud. When they returned, Lionel helped Stanley to the door

with a healthy share of sea bream and
mackerel. Mrs Carelli was there waiting.

'Ah, thank you,' she began.
'I guess we won't be short of
fish for the week.'

'No problem,' replied Lionel. 'I told you we'd make a fisherman of this lad.'

'Oh and thank you for the flowers, Mister Grouse.'

'Er … no problem. You're very welcome.' Lionel eyed Stanley, who was concealing a grin.

That night it had turned unusually cold. Mrs Carelli knew the fishing trip had frozen Stanley to the bone, so she sat him in front of the fire. He curled up like a cat with a huge blanket around him, drinking from a steaming mug.

'You don't need to tell me you had good fortune today, Stanley, and I ain't talking about no fishing neither. Unless of course you counts fish that makes a nuisance of themselves and gets what they deserves.' Mrs Carelli sat and stared into the fire.

When she disapproved, she didn't look at him whilst she spoke to him. But deep down he knew she was happy.

Rightly or wrongly, Stanley and Mr Grouse had solved a few big problems for Crampton Rock.

'Don't forget, Stanley. Whilst you're here, I'm your guardian. And if you're up to no good it looks bad on me. So keep your heroic wild adventures under your hat, will you?'

'Will do, Mrs C. Er … how did you know we weren't just fishing?'

'I ain't known you long, lad, but I know this much. It takes more than a day's fishing to get you out of your bed at five o'clock of a morning.' For a moment, he thought she'd finished, but she carried on. 'And you can forget about this Ibis business. Tain't nowhere I can see it and I've cleaned every nook and

171

cranny there is. This old place has got some dark secrets, Stanley, but you're best ignoring 'em unless you want to dig yourself into deeper trouble. You'll be going home to your parents soon so you'd best get it out of your head, lad.'

And then, as if to show him that she secretly admired his heroics, she went to the kitchen and returned with a fantastic-looking pie. He hadn't felt this hungry in ages, and set about demolishing it with a skill that was to be respected.

'That's the boy I know,' she laughed.

She sat back in the chair and fell asleep, as outside the crazy world of Crampton Rock turned dark – and the doors stayed unbolted.

The Pike again

Home! Stanley hadn't thought of home for some time. It was a world away.

But for now his time at Crampton Rock had come to an end, and he must return to the mundane way of life he had forgotten about.

'Stanley, I shall leave you in peace to say goodbye to the house.' Off to do her shopping, Mrs Carelli left him with a hug.

173

'I'll be waiting at the harbour to wave you farewell. Mister Grouse will walk you back along the wooden mile.'

Stanley sat and stared at his favourite view. The sea rolled back and forth, and he knew that whenever he returned it would always be there. He thought of all he had been through in such a short time. The tiniest tear welled up in his eye and he let it roll down his cheek until it disappeared.

He spotted a bird on the corner of the roof, and suddenly his thoughts turned to the Ibis. Stanley's preoccupation with pirates had kept his curiosity at bay, but now that Crampton Rock was free again he had begun to wonder.

Stanley could have looked for the Ibis, but he hadn't. He'd explored the house already and though he had found much, he had certainly not found anything that could be it. Perhaps it was buried in the grave of his pirate great-uncle. Maybe it lay somewhere at the bottom of the vast ocean, amongst the rocks and corals. Could it be in the cellar or the roof space? Maybe. Another time, perhaps; too many adventures all at once would be bad for him.

Anyway, his case was packed and waiting on the bed. It was time to hit home. Mrs Carelli would be looking after the old place through the autumn, and he would return in the winter.

His train was due in an hour.

He made his way to the front door, plonking his case under the hat stand. Remembering the bracing walk along slimy planks, he wrapped up well. Tracing his hands around the insides of his pockets, he discovered the letter he had never posted to his mother.

But on the point of opening the door, Stanley decided he had to do one last thing. He couldn't forget the dream he'd had, or the words of his old friend the pike.

He ran to the kitchen, grabbed a butter knife, then raced down the corridor to where the case was fixed upon the wall. Taking the round-ended blade, he used it to unscrew the glass and reveal the pike. For the first time he was right up close to it. Somehow it seemed almost alive, more real than behind the glass that protected it.

Stanley brought a chair and stood on it so he could get even closer. He ran a hand over the smooth surface of the pike's scaly body, and touched the pin-like points of its teeth, as the words came back to him.

'Fear not, Stanley. When you are gone, I shall hold your secret safely.'

With his head pressed up against the case, Stanley looked down, deep into the pike's open mouth. And he saw something. In the hollowed-out body of the fish, something winked back at him with a glint of light. His heart leaped.

'Don't touch her, Stanley, let her be.'

It was the first time Stanley had heard the pike in a long while. But it was too late to heed the warning. He was too eager and had already reached inside, cutting his wrist on the needled points of the teeth.

The shining silver prize was in his hand.

'Worry not, Mister Pike,' said Stanley.
'I shall be careful.'

He moved towards the window to examine
it more closely. It held the perfect shape of
a wading bird. with a long curved beak,
positioned in a stooping
pose, as if searching for
something through the
water. It was the most
beautiful thing he had
ever seen and though
he thought he might be
imagining it, he felt a strange force, a kind of
power, pumping like a beating heart.

'The Ibis,' he whispered.

'Come on, Stanley Buggles. Train is
a-waiting.' Mrs Carelli was back, and her
sharp shrill made him jump.

Quickly, he replaced it. Just as it was.
He fastened the glass and returned the knife.

'Thank you, pike,' he said. 'I shall see you in the winter.'

He picked up his case, locked the door and made his way down to the harbour. A smile broke across his face as he turned and said goodbye to the place he had come to love.

Back indoors, the pike made a delicate twitch and its body moved ever so slightly in the glass case. For a short moment it felt sure that its heart was beginning to beat. A brief wisp of life rippled through it. And then as suddenly as it had started, it stopped.

And just for now, that was all that happened.

Chris Mould

Chris Mould went to art school at the age of sixteen. During this time, he did various jobs, from delivering papers to washing-up and cooking in a kitchen. He has won the Nottingham Children's Book Award and been commended for the Sheffield. He loves his work and likes to write and draw the kind of books that he would have liked to have on his shelf as a boy. He is married with two children and lives in Yorkshire.

All looks crisp and cosy in
Crampton Rock as Stanley Buggles
settles down for the winter.
But something wicked has blown
in with the wind.

What is the **headless ghost**
of Admiral Swift desperate to tell Stanley?

And who are the *deadly pirates*,
marching through the oncoming blizzard ...?

Are you prepared to be scared?

This book contains ten of the most terrifying tales, adapted, written and superbly illustrated by award-winner

Five are original ghost stories, and five are retellings of classic tales, from *The Legend of Sleepy Hollow* by Washington Irving to *The Tell-Tale Heart* by Edgar Allen Poe.

Open this book at your own peril ...